DEATH BENEFITS

DEATH BENEFITS

A CENTURY OF SONNETS

DAVID R. SLAVITT

Louisiana State University Press
BATON ROUGE

Published by Louisiana State University Press
lsupress.org

Copyright © 2024 by David Slavitt
All rights reserved. Except in the case of brief quotations used in articles or reviews, no part of this publication may be reproduced or transmitted in any format or by any means without written permission of Louisiana State University Press.

LSU Press Paperback Original

Designer: Kaelin Chappell Broaddus
Typefaces: Dolly Pro, text; Bebas Neue, and Gotham, display.

Cover image courtesy AdobeStock/Tori

Library of Congress Cataloging-in-Publication Data

Names: Slavitt, David R., 1935– author.
Title: Death benefits : a century of sonnets / David R. Slavitt.
Description: Baton Rouge : Louisiana State University Press, 2024.
Identifiers: LCCN 2024010859 (print) | LCCN 2024010860 (ebook) | ISBN 978-0-8071-8255-0 (paperback) | ISBN 978-0-8071-8348-9 (epub) | ISBN 978-0-8071-8349-6 (pdf)
Subjects: LCGFT: Poetry.
Classification: LCC PS3569.L3 D43 2024 (print) | LCC PS3569.L3 (ebook) | DDC 811/.54—dc23/eng/20240311
LC record available at https://lccn.loc.gov/2024010859
LC ebook record available at https://lccn.loc.gov/2024010860

IN MEMORIAM:
George Garrett,
Kelly Cherry,
Richard Dillard,
Brendan Galvin,
and Fred Chappell

DEATH BENEFITS

1

A paragraph signals a pause; a more emphatic
break you can indicate with an extra space;
stronger yet, you can start the following line
in bold face—to congratulate the reader
for having reached this milestone. It is a goal
because he could not help taking notice
that a little down the page were darker letters.
(Does he suppose he now deserves a rest?)

Childish. But aren't all punctuation marks
condescending? Can we admit that we need
such prompts without losing face? Confess
that we remain dependent on the help
the cantillation of grammar offers beginners.
And we are always beginners, again and again.

2

An assertive dropped initial raises its voice
as we have been taught never to do unless
there is a fire in that crowded theater.
But poems' theaters are never crowded. So?
Do as you like. Nobody cares anyway.
I was in the Bluebird reading group,
swifter than Grackles and Sparrows. (There were no Swifts
or Dodos, who weren't bright but understood insults.)

But to be a Bluebird came at a cost we discovered
only later and are still paying: were they
the luckier ones after all, surrounded
as they have always seemed to be by buddies
they drink beer and bowl with? Do I think so?
I hope not, but, drinking alone, I wonder.

3

Socrates taught us all how little we know,
playing gotcha with his Athenian pals
none of whom could describe the world they lived in.
They weren't blind or stupid, but Socrates's tricks
of logic tripped them up time after time.
All it would have taken was nerve to see
that the subject was always the shortcomings of thinking.
Crito, Phaedo, and all the rest should have known

that the only way to win was not to play.
Words don't get us anywhere. Or worse,
they deceive us, making us doubt what's there
before our puzzled eyes. The skeptics knew
that laughter persists, and tears and groans of pain.
We have no need for trivial specification.

4

Even if it makes no sense, one must
believe in something. Which will I run out of
first, money or time? The ups and downs
of the market hint at how much or how little
I can afford to think about: upticks
mean health like a good blood glucose number.
Peering down into the canyons of zero
I guess I can survive, living on cat food

(which is more expensive than it used to be).
When I was little, monsters lurked in the darkness
of the closet or under the bed. I lay still,
hoping they might not notice me. They were real,
but over the years they have begun to fade
as I have too, becoming less and less so.

5

Pistols make noise ... But would I hear it?
Lightning strikes; the thunder comes later.
Anyway, where would I get a gun? Those louche
parts of town, where men in the shadows ask
no questions, are dangerous. You could get killed,
saving yourself trouble and money, too.
Messy, but in a tiled, hotel bathroom
chambermaids would deal with it. (Tip well!)

Rooftops and the leap from thought to action
are more attractive. The fall, while it lasts, will be
thrilling beyond thought. The terror will offer
a definitive truth, an answer to all questions.
You don't have to be smart. All that's required
is need and, for an instant, bravery.

6

Writers kill themselves, not all but enough:
Virginia Woolf and Hemingway, and Mishima,
Stefan Zweig, Kawabata, Hart Crane,
Mayakovsky, Celan, Schnitzler, Pavese,
Sylvia Plath, Anne Sexton, Primo Levi,
and . . . aposiopesis (a sentence breaking off).
Literature is supposed to explain life's
incoherences, but it doesn't, does it?

These writers came to realize this and found
that it undid what they had spent their lives at.
What other way could they imagine to frame
an answer to the rude and impossible question?
Defy it? Try to evade it? It won't go away,
and the fiction, dissolving, leaves us in eerie silence.

7

Circular staircases and chandeliers
are badges of wealth and its extravagant comforts.
Their invitations to suicide are displays
of defiance. Having survived, ignoring them,
our burghers and our betters are proud of themselves
for their self-satisfaction that thrives like kudzu.
But do we have the right to condescend
or criticize them? (Yes, but only in whispers.)

Faith that never wavers is mere habit
serious people question. Only electric
candles never flicker or gutter. Doubt
is an authentication you have to earn
in struggles to the death. Or you can concede,
preserving your honor, if such a thing exists.

8

As writing seems less attractive, one turns
away to another opposite medium:
erasure that can conquer the pest past.
Io oblivisco, a proud motto, proclaims
your new freedom from imperfect ideas
of what may have happened and all the misleading lessons
you've learned. The nihilist studies negative numbers
that a series of zeros manages to avoid.

To anticipate the weather's wearing away
of letters, leave the stone blank or, better,
put only a proofreader's sign "delete"—
the horizontal line with a loop at the end,
like a tired gallows noose, taking it easy,
lying down for a bit, like you beneath it.

9

To stop writing is perilous. Late mornings
are the worst time. You can't just scribble letters
to friends (most are dead). And it's hard to pretend
to literature. Just type? The quick, brown fox
waits to raid your mental chicken-coop.
I should be better equipped after all those years
of pretending an audience, however small—
readers who were, in both senses, curious.

It builds. One morning's *schmertz* expands to include
all those other mornings, days, years
of a solipsism that has been lately rent
to allow me glimpses through its veil, hints
of what we call the real world. (I don't
trust it, but I have no other options.)

10

Some books pretend, or we pretend
to have read them or to be reading. The coffee table
sports Ludwig Wittgenstein's *Tractatus
Logico-Philosophicus*. Does it become
fictional? (Is it any less demanding?)
To drop Ludwig's name is easier still,
and he changes for a moment into a context.
He spoke of the "language-game," which seems to include

everything: contexts endow words
with meanings. An intellectual woman I knew
took her time deciding what book to wear,
that is, to carry with her for its effect,
to accessorize her mood of that day. Some
she had read, but that made little difference.

11

Pockets: no longer having to carry things
in their hands gave women significant freedom.
Progress. But there are always risks. I think
of Virginia Woolf gathering those stones
to put in her pockets to keep what would be her corpse
from embarrassment, floating up to the surface.
Considerate? Possibly prudish? I resist
the literary temptation to give each stone

import as if it were another dismal
thought, a further burden in her despair.
But no, they were just insignificant stones
a writer's habit betrays with a fancied meaning—
that could have been a part of her disgust,
the loss of an honesty she sometimes remembered.

12

Spoiler alerts warn off the wrong readers,
who think that a book is its plot and cannot imagine
why else one would read it. How do the lovers
manage to get together? Does the villain
die? Is virtue rewarded, wickedness punished?
Fiction is a fiction, which is to say
it isn't at all like that in the world, so truth
itself is a spoiler from which only a few

are able or willing to learn. Most people
(not unwashed but not quite literate either)
prefer reassurance and comfort, however mendacious.
Do not try to correct them. We battle, outnumbered
and overwhelmed, but they refuse to see
how "Let there be light" also implies darkness.

13

We used to read to learn what the world is like,
what other people are like—if not answers,
hints, a nudge in the right direction. But writers
conspire never to be of any help.
They are even offended when we turn
their art into a crude *vade mecum*.
What machines come with a guarantee
that they won't work, or if, somehow, they do,

we can get a refund? Truth disappoints.
Reality, being everywhere around us,
is a random jumble, unsurprising, while we
dream of something better or, anyway, different.
After those dreams have died, we read to admire
the artifice, having become connoisseurs.

14

While Friedrich Rüchert, the eminent scholar, was working
on Ethiopic grammar, swatting it up
greedily, the large bookshelves behind him
collapsed and poured down on his head the weighty
volumes he had lived with—and crushed him to death.
Irony? No, look again but harder,
and let us suppose for a moment that all that knowledge
entered his brain at once lighting up his cortex.

May we not allow ourselves a moment
to toy with the idea of his life's work
filling his appetitive spirit's yawning
maw, not in heaven, but here, if only
briefly, answering all his polyglot prayers
including those he hadn't had time to frame?

15

The Four Seasons in Philadelphia looks
like the others in the chain. They're all nowhere,
but this one has a slender thread connecting,
albeit awkwardly, to a time and place.
At the front desk ask them in which room
Joan Rivers's husband committed suicide.
You'll get that fish-eye hotel clerks are good at,
but not an answer. They may not even know

the whole story—how, four days before,
Joan had announced she wanted a separation.
That same week, her psychiatrist also
killed himself. (They're not immune.) That hotel room
briefly checked into the real world, violating
the decorum of the chain's fantasy land.

16

Shrouds are good manners, for none of the ghosts
wishes to seem to preen. Rich and poor
face God in uniform winding sheets
with belts tied to resemble the Hebrew letter
shin (the initial of one of God's names, or a dreidel's
losing letter). But God is never fooled:
he sees naked souls and how they have fared.
What limits us is our inadequate

imaginations that cannot comprehend
the sea of souls that stretches into the distance,
frightening but also reassuring.
We will join that enormous miscellany,
who in their anonymity take comfort,
as pebbles appear to do on a sunlit shingle.

17

If all magicians are fakes, the best of them
are the truest fakes, or say at least the boldest,
daring us to believe in what we know
cannot possibly be. He pulls from his hat
the rabbit of course, but then, right away, the toad.
And Marianne Moore? And Helen Vendler,
who bursts into multicolored flames. (Applause—
from the audience, especially English majors.)

But let us imagine an actual miracle: who
could tell the difference? Prestidigitation
is too easy an answer (but mostly correct).
Jesus turns water into wine, produces
endless loaves and fishes—and there is applause,
disappointing, insulting, but better than nothing.

18

Graffiti artists, unlikely theoreticians,
sign blank walls and highway overpasses
not claiming the structures as their artworks,
which are the signatures themselves. Or is this
only an intermediate step? Workmen
will come with whitewash. Afterwards the art
will survive, morphing into its photographs
and then to the thought to which the picture refers,

for maintenance cannot obliterate ideas.
They fade, but so do frescoes and pastels.
What the mind can retain is all that will last,
as art imitates life, or one could say
comes to life and suffers vicissitudes:
Close your eyes and see the graffito shimmer.

19

Stage fright poses impertinent, pertinent questions
about those claims of merit performance makes.
Who do you think you are? What can you say
or do worth people's attention? That flash
of doubt you try so hard to hide or deny
is legitimate. The choice is between pretense
and stupidity (or, with more tact, delusion).
But how can I unpublish what I've written,

go back to the beginning, and leave the pens
and keyboards untouched as they were before
my vanity first imposed itself upon them?
Virgil on his deathbed gave instructions
that his *Aeneid* be burned. This modest judgment
indicts the rest of us: we are all guilty.

20

The Grand Guignol in Paris closed its doors
in 1962: the competition
of the world's horrors eclipsed them. The director,
Charles Nonon (No, no kidding!) admitted
that "We could never equal Buchenwald."
One of its best productions was *Un crime
dans une maison de fous*. We live there now,
all of us, and there's no Emergency Exit.

Never mind what depresses depressives
or drives maniacs mad. It is the normal,
stupid, self-centered, and oblivious people
we must worry about. Where is the cure
for them? Boethius? Or Dostoievsky?
Beyond words; even beyond silence.

21

Painting = paint, canvas, and brushes;
writing = pens, paper, and ink.
Beyond that is a leap into the unlikely
and arrogant—a kinder word would be
"foolish." We proclaim ourselves magicians.
Does this mean that? Does this even mean this?
The blindfolds over our eyes are pain and desire:
together they prompt belief in our own tricks

at least for the moment. (We dare not ask for more.)
Then the stage goes dark and we descend
into the dimness, having to bid farewell
yet again to our dreams and beloved dead.
We envy our audiences, who do not care
and thus can avoid our dreadful disillusion.

22

You're reading along and you come across a word
you've never seen before (or have forgotten?).
The context doesn't help. Should you now bother
to look it up? A good habit to have,
but every day there is less and less point.
Will you ever use the word? Or see it again?
On the other hand, not to walk five steps
to the dictionary would be to admit defeat,

a trivial loss but one that keeps on growing.
So go, mush the dogsled to Fort Despair
to learn the rare and useless word: *caduke*
("ephemeral" or "not quite obsolete").
That's what you get for being the good boy
you used to think you ought to want to be.

23

Concentrate on your breathing. After a time
(you will know when) you will be paying attention
more to the stillnesses between the breaths—
the thousands every day, from which we learn
nothing, distracted by our flittering thoughts.
A cat, crouched near a mouse hole, motionless,
doesn't have these. You should emulate its
empty mind that you can barely imagine.

Mystics aspire to blackness beyond blackness
and stare at the sun until they go blind and can see
the darkness that is the converse of all light.
Consider the night with which the light is pregnant.
Words fail, but you are far beyond them
with their distortions of focus and constraint.

24

A skein is a sixth of a hank, but that is not
helpful. Simple equivalents, please. But these
vary, which is confusing. With cotton, for instance,
a skein is eight and a quarter yards. Not so
with tapestry wool (ten yards) or crewel wool
(thirty-three yards). Better, beat a retreat
to the ignorance with which we all began.
Metaphors, at any rate, do not

require specificity. Wool-gathering
has no minimum quantity. At length
(whatever length that is) one moves on
to the next pointless project. To keep up his spirits,
he tries to adjust his mind, avoid thinking,
and keep to his knitting, for surely the cold is coming.

25

After I've peed in the morning, I have to decide
whether to go back to bed or dress
and go to the desk in the study—a minor matter,
but it indicates the day's balance of habit
and inclination in what is a moral measure
and one of depression. The solid desk pretends
that I am not yet catatonic. (I know it's pretense
because I am the pretender.) Call it a fiction

I hope may somehow come true. Do jeans and a T-shirt
count, even without shoes and socks?
Who knows? If the dead were able to change their shrouds
for coats and ties, might they move with us
and pass among us as living, encouraging us,
still breathing and able to make choices?

26

Are rats ever wrong, abandoning sound
vessels for no good reason, leaving them cleansed?
Like them, my words are fleeing, perhaps to swim
free and take their chances, leaving me
the infant I was, whimpering, squalling, waiting
for the world's vocabulary to assemble
and come aboard, to infest and enlighten (corrupt?)
my self's mute self. I have supposed

that he has been lurking for years now, for decades,
sure that he would return to the captain's cabin
and without a word reassume command.
That moment has come at last, as I knew it would,
and I am of course speechless but not unprepared.
I was like this once; it wasn't so bad.

27

Doubt is not your enemy: learn to embrace it
so that you can feel its warm breath
on your neck. Paradoxically, it can even
help you in your work, humbled and freed.
Worthlessness excuses imperfections,
and nobody cares. Rely on that indifference
to do as you please. You may discover by luck
or instinct what intention had concealed.

Fools sometimes realize they are holy
although they never aimed for holiness
(which was unlikely, as even fools know).
But calculation and prudence are beyond them—
or on the contrary beneath them. A fool's
paradise is the only one there is.

28

How can I trust my friends' approval? What else
can they possibly say? I have no way of knowing
how much of what they tell me is good manners
or sentiment. Kindly deceit is still
deceit, and even honesty is suspect.
Worse than that, they may truly believe
what they have written or said on the telephone,
disposed, as they are, to like what they have read.

A friendly eye may choose to turn blind;
I must rely therefore on total strangers,
or, better, one of those whom I have slighted
or offended and who begrudge me any attention,
never mind the tepid, grudging praise
I can extort from them: my audience.

29

Thousands, tens of thousands have given up
efforts at writing. For most of them it was
the right decision it took too long to make.
They have their dog-eared manuscripts in a drawer
or up on a closet shelf. But few of them tell us
how it feels to sit at a desk no longer.
How could they, without sitting down again
to do what they have resolved not to do anymore?

Anyone who tried would be a liar
like the famous Cretan in Epimenides's
clever riddle, in which case, I admit
that I, too, am lying, but I am telling
you the truth. At least I am trying to,
or would be, if there were any such thing.

30

We learn words first and then the grammar,
making mistake after mistake until
some adult (benevolent, one hopes)
inculcates a new habit: *John is as tall
as Bill but not so tall as Philip*. We wince
whenever we hear the wrong conjunction in
negative comparisons. The rule,
engraved deeply enough, is what we become.

What we must then learn is more difficult:
toleration, patience, and forbearance.
Dearer than intelligence, these are efforts
at virtue, although quick minds can hide
faltering spirits. But ask any looking glass
whether you do any better than vampires?

31

"*Risus sardonicus*" refers to the facial convulsions
caused by tetanus or strychnine, the "evil-
looking grin" that also comes from ingesting
water-dropwort that has the right neurotoxin.
Years ago, in Sardinia, old men and women,
no longer self-supporting, would be given
a drink of that plant's intoxicating juice
and then, when they were drunk, thrown off a cliff

to the rocks below. Could "*sardonicus*" also
refer to the Sardinians' euthanasia?
(If we choose to think so, who will object?)
The grin, like those who show it, is short lived,
but those few seconds are enough for the thought
to cross the mind and mercifully distract it.

32

A writer's silence is different from anyone else's.
His is earned while other men and women
are hardly bothered by any hiatus of language.
We must concentrate on holding our tongues
even when others talk or write and we
disagree or want to correct an error.
Some monastic orders disdain speech
as if it were the devil's work. It's not,

but neither is it the angels'. Holiness
may be the goal, but quiet concentrates
and distracts (in equal measure). A gate, agape,
beckons and terrifies. We are the moths
aflutter about the heart of its dark candle,
imagining our moment of ultimate silence.

33

German was Paul Celan's *Muttersprache*,
which is to say the *Sprache* you mutter in.
He hated it, or anyway the taste
of ashes it left in his mouth no matter what
words he said. (His father died of typhus
in a camp in Transnistria; his mother
was shot in the neck.) Clench your teeth on that,
as he must have done all the damnable time.

The closest thing to silence is warped speech,
violations of syntax, deliberate
neologisms, random syllables.
He was confined in a Parisian loony bin,
the only sane man in France. *Natürlich.*
A misunderstanding. He had to kill himself.

34

Where should a novel stop? How and when?
Whatever end you settle on should make
a significant comment on what has gone before,
as an elegy does or an obit. Your outlined plot
hardly matters. Stories end whenever
they want to or have to. Writers control
the necessities, having freedoms the characters don't—
limited by the inherent falsification

all fictions depend on: that there is meaning,
or any discernible order to events
or behavior. You must try to avoid bald-faced
lies. Let your readers collaborate
and share your guilt. It's only a misdemeanor
if no one realizes that he has been hurt.

35

Bad habits are hard enough to break,
even with guilt as your unruly helper;
the good ones are harder: camouflaged as virtue,
they demand that you revise your ideas
of good and evil, develop new instincts,
and assume, another, better identity.
But can you concede that your life up until now
has been a misunderstanding, a mistake?

The ghosts of those misspent years haunt you,
imploring, nagging, or merely sulking in silence.
Is it so stupid to sit at the desk again,
imagining readers paying attention? The ghosts
wheedle and offer implausible reassurance—
that you were right and the rest of the world was wrong.

36

An audience—an interview with a pope
or a king. Or your readers. The word changes
although the spelling remains the same. But think
how courtiers scrutinized the facial expressions
and shifting moods of Ivan the Terrible, Pedro
the Cruel, or Baldric the Mediocre. Read them
aright and one prospered in wealth or rank,
could sit in the presence, or enter the privy chamber.

Our audiences, too, have high-stakes power,
volatile beings we have to please. But how?
We hazard expensive guesses. Are they crazy?
We study to be like them. The alternative
is going back home, which means giving up
on the daydream we had of someday fixing the roof.

37

How do those dragons guarding their treasure know
that gold is rare and therefore precious? Do some
keep watch over chests heaping with nickels and dimes
or telephone jetons from foreign countries?
Ugly raptors in branches of nearby trees
assume that the dragons know what they are doing
and screech warnings to errant and erroneous
knights that happen by. The vigilant beasts

and their chests with stones and metals are mere conventions
we have agreed to. Do not ask rude questions
or look away: the system would collapse
and the world we trust turn as dark as the woods
of the picturesque folktales we tell grandchildren,
whose fears we share but have learned to keep hidden.

38

Writers invent things. It comes with the job.
Still, they are bound by certain constraints that refer
to the real world readers think they live in
and its probabilities. For a greater freedom
you have to look up on a dark, starry night
and imagine what astrophysicists dream up.
Is there a planet, the size of a ping-pong ball
that weighs as much as the earth, a powerful dwarf

way out there, nudging the others' orbits?
Our radio-telescopes cannot pick it up,
but some professor writes on a blackboard crowded
with numbers and arcane symbols, and there is applause
from the learnèd men and women in the hall,
persuaded that what they see may be the truth.

39

Not noble. Just an attempt to escape
the repetitiveness of our lives, the metaphysical
ennui that surrounds us. Literature
doesn't need another sentence: the books
already on the shelves are enough to last
the rest of even the longest lives, but reading
is not what we hunger for. Diversion
is never enough. Therefore, the choice is between

the pen and the pistol to fend off the torment
of forever brushing and flossing, setting the table
and then washing the dishes . . . The gun makes more
noise but lasts longer. Which you pick
depends on the thinness your patience has been worn to
and what level your disgust has reached.

40

The day always began with yesterday's work
that I'd go over, scanning for any typos,
or infelicities I hadn't noticed
but now glare. Here and there I'd change
a word or recast a sentence to make it less
ungainly, although each correction hurt,
indicting me for lapses of attention
or, what is worse, general ineptness?

The idea was to ease into the day
but where is that assurance I need now?
I go ahead, despite myself. It is all
in spite and chastened. Rilke said that you must
change your life. But can you change it back?
Or, if you cannot change it, should you end it?

41

I can remember how the growing pile
of pages gave weight to my dream of a book.
There it was for me to make it neat,
aligning it by tapping it on the desk.
At the least, what I held in my hand
was now harder to discard and admit
I had been playing charades. The wastebasket
had to yawn wider now to wake me.

The fiction had metamorphosed, fictional now,
having grow that two-letter suffix. Did God
never doubt his work? After that first
"Let there be light," did he hesitate
a nanosecond and add, "Or maybe not"
because of the faults in his draft universe?

42

To be a writer! I used to think that made me
special. Yes, but not if you allow
fantasies—or delusions—to qualify
as fictions: everyone else on the trolley car
is a mental writer who doesn't need fountain pens.
They bear with greater or lesser grace burdens
as engaging as any of Flaubert's or Tolstoy's.
Whatever I can see through the rain-streaked window

I turn into material. My own face
is a blur; to clarify it would be a distortion.
None of my fellow passengers needs to worry
about such nuances. Can I reform
and learn to live as they all seem to do?
No, but I am able to pretend.

43

Refinement? Sensitivity? In a pig's
pizzazza! Think of what they have to endure
from the deluge of rejections that are all
ambiguous. (Do they apply to the work or the person?
And should one attempt to disambiguate?)
Writers have to be thugs to suffer the boorish
behavior of editors and committee members
who pass them over for fellowships, prizes, and grants.

How can one sustain the absurd idea
he must believe—that he is right and the world
is wrong? In time the spirit's carapace
will show some craquelure or disintegrate
entirely. Brave or stupid, he must decide
whether or not to persist in his nightmare.

44

"Truth to tell" is awkward, as it should be,
the phrase and the activity, too. Who wants
to hear that time cures only some wounds
and often incompletely? There's scar tissue,
the cicatrix. (It isn't a kind of bird,
dangerous and probably endangered.)
A disfigurement. Or a badge your body bears
to commemorate what happened, i.e. your life?

Lesser cuts and bruises you forget,
most of whatever you have had to endure;
the more serious insults leave behind
dense masses of tough fibrous tissue
that in distracted moments your finger can palpate
to remind you who you were and are still.

45

I am pretending to write, or do I pretend
to pretend, hoping that what I'm doing is real?
Pretense can be a career. There is a Count
of Paris who plays at being the King of France.
When I was young, the pretender styled himself
as Henri VII; his son was Jean IV,
condemned to this charade, the Orléanist claimant.
(There were others, the Bourbons and Bonapartists.)

Their friends conspired with them as marquises and dukes,
and addressed one another with the old,
grandiose titles they had come to believe in.
I am on my own, with no coterie
to support me in maintaining my delusions
as I assert my claim to be an ex-writer.

46

Trollope's greatest fiction was the one
he told himself—that he could stop anytime.
Get up from the desk? Go for a walk and observe
the trees coming into leaf? Not so easy,
for he was no longer master but galley slave,
chained to a bench, pulling his heavy oar.
He could have claimed once to be making a living,
but not towards the end, when the "rewards" had become

punishments or, certainly, disincentives.
The choices are clearer for me than they were for Tony,
even though it took me years to see them.
Rehabilitation is difficult
unless addicts can keep their disgust sharp—
as the booze, or meth, or fentanyl. Or writing.

47

Texts only seem to refer to something
else: they are, *faute de mieux,* their own
subject. Dying words, for instance, mean
he is alive, still thinking. What about?
It hardly matters. There is no *mieux* anymore.
What the French locution when their mood
is baroque is *"Faute de grives, on mange des merles."*
Lacking thrushes one must eat blackbirds.

Do poor children complain, "Blackbirds again?"
Lacking chickens do they fall back on turkey?
Wanting peacocks do they dine on penguins?
Albatrosses and vultures? Ostrich and emu?
When the time comes, can I remember that
as my defiant and absurd last words?

48

Was it Jeremy Bentham or John Stuart Mill
who coined the phrase about the greatest good
for the greatest number? Who knows? And who cares?
It isn't true. Gifford Pinchot tweaked it
to make it a little less silly by adding
"in the long run." (He ran the Forest Service
and had learned patience watching trees grow.)
The problem is, when you make any decision,

you have to know what other parties are thinking.
And you can't. Ever. You're not even sure they exist,
except as figments, robots made to annoy you.
Assume they are real and you, too, are a robot.
Kant warns against this. Leibnitz is less
clear: his nomad monads now provoke laughter.

49

On the one hand, the executives running Ford,
some of whom had taken English and knew
that Marianne Moore was somebody important—
not that they'd ever read or understood
or enjoyed poems of hers, or, for that matter,
anyone else—but they were cautious and prudent,
and believed in market research and asking experts
to find something more trustworthy, more real

than their own whims. Why not consult the poet
herself? So, on the other hand, there's Moore:
Mongoose Civique? Turcotingo? Jesus!
A joke? No? Which was more insulting?
Back in the real world they settled on *Edsel*—
awful, but at least everybody agreed.

50

I had given her up, but she persists—
to annoy me, or break my heart. Either way
she had me at her merciless hello.
What she does is prompt me with ideas
that, if I were open for business, would be attractive.
What will I do? Quit trying to quit?
She'll teach me a thing or two. (Is there ever
a second thing? Or, for that matter, a first?)

It's no secret. Every Lothario knows
how indifference, real or feigned, can provoke
interest, perhaps present a challenge. The muse
(not mine anymore), irked or piqued,
behaves as women will, and sends these ideas
to tempt me. Poker-faced, I try to ignore her.

51

Is there any difference between writing
and pretending to write? Doesn't the answer depend
on what is in the mind of the man or woman
sitting at the desk and entering words
on a keyboard that, of course, cannot distinguish
between the chalk and the cheese? And the intention
can change at any moment. Throw it away?
Put it in the closet? Submit it somewhere?

Over time the question may answer itself
(as I may or may not realize):
are these pages authentic or oneiric?
The world will make its decision after I'm dead,
but while I'm alive I can't help venturing guesses,
as I do all the time with everything else.

52

Anna, Dostoevsky's second wife,
had to put up with a lot. Writers' wives
often do, but in any competition
she'd be a prime contender. Poverty
is, in itself, inconvenient. Worse
is when you have been reduced to nothing because
your idiot-genius husband again lost
what little he had and more at the card table.

I read that she had to pawn her underwear.
For how much? How little? Is there a coin
smaller than a kopek? What pawnbroker
would bother, except as a kindness to the lady?
His novels are depressing but nothing to this
fabulous and melodramatic transaction.

53

Weightlessness is a diminution of being.
There are a number of saints who could levitate
and hover high in the air of church naves,
amazing the congregations, who believed
and took it as a mark of sinlessness.
But rise above the literal and consider
that glimpse of innocence in their raised eyes,
however brief. Had he felt the burden

of human sin lift from his aching shoulders?
Could he ascend higher, like the angels,
even to Heaven's gate? But what if he felt
a twinge of doubt at fifty thousand feet,
a hesitation? Would that minutest defect
result in his fatal plummet back to earth?

54

Ah, Percy, Percy, how do you feel
now about your sonnet they teach in grade school
because it is simple enough for the nine-year-olds
(and the teachers, too, few of whom read poems
ever for pleasure)? Poor Ozymandias! Famous
no more, and isn't that sad? No, not very.
His monument stands out there in the glaring desert's
"lone and level sands." (How are they "lone"?

The first one-syllable word you could think of
and settled for?) I never asked. The teacher
knew I was a wise-ass and would have sent me
to the principal's office again to be lectured to.
Boring, inelegant, it would have done no good
and wouldn't have explained the lone sands either.

55

"Better coffee a Rockefeller's money can't buy"
used to be a line in the Chock full o'Nuts
jingle. But the Rockefellers threatened
to sue, and Cf o'N caved and made it
"a millionaire's money," disimproving the line
but saving legal fees. It wasn't true!
What about Jamaica Blue or Rwanda
Izuba (they harvest the beans at night to avoid

gunfire)? Or Kopi Luwak, the coffee
from Indonesia? (The beans pass through
the gastrointestinal tract of a palm civet
to enhance the flavor.) Rockefellers prefer it
if only because their guests have no idea
what's in the delicate porcelain cups before them.

56

Among the many reasons not to write
are the excellent books already on the shelves
(many the writer has never read or heard of).
Even if he lives as long as trees do,
he won't have time for them all, to learn from them
and delight in their pages. To add to this pile?
Arrogance, delusion, and vainglory!
The keyboard displays its teeth in a steady rictus,

not of amusement but smirking. How can he bear it?
What he admits—worse than stupidity—
is deplorable taste. Outside my window, a crow
thinks it is singing. Does it love the sound
of its own voice and those of other crows?
Get up from the desk. Now, go to the bookcase.

57

Kleist had been thinking about killing himself
(writers immolate themselves in metaphor
every day) and was working up to it
when he met Fraulein Vogel, who preferred
to die by her own hand than let her cancer
do its slow, messy work. They discussed
nostricide, a solution to their problems:
he could simply shoot her and then, to evade

the executioner's sword (that's how they did it
back then), he'd have to kill himself, too.
The king and queen of the Romantic Movement?
Or were they merely efficient technicians? They have
a trolley stop now, so people can visit the site
and the stone commemorating whatever it was.

58

A manuscript remains passive until
the writer lets it fly from his desk to those
of others, where it comes to active life,
an agent now beyond its author's reach.
With most of us, that's as far as it goes,
but the big guys, the "major" poets endure
and begin to take themselves seriously—
a *Complete Poems*, with notes, the scholars' delight

where they can show off, no longer subservient,
but exhibiting a mastery over the text
that amounts to ownership. In a variorum
edition, the scraps and orts from his wastebasket
demonstrate the editor's taste and the writer's
luck—a useful idiot at best.

59

We can endure most disappointments, losses,
even catastrophes, but there is a last
straw that is just too much and undoes the camel.
Suicide then seems to be the only
reasonable choice. After each day's
work, God is said to have said, "Good."
But what if it hadn't been quite good enough?
Would he have destroyed it? Utterly?

(Does he ever do anything by halves?)
Not writing lifts a heavy burden,
but I am less, diminished, floating away.
Is what remains worth remaining for?
Out of habit or cowardice? Or is it
laziness, the worst and likeliest reason?

60

What do you do with a royalty check for ZERO
AND 25/100 DOLLARS, worth
more as a reminder of who you are
than if you cash it? It comes from a decent press,
or rather its computers' algorithms.
It isn't enough to have paid for its metered postage
but here it is, an eloquent message from fate
to inflict upon you that hard lesson you needed

to be reviewed, drilled into your head.
You cannot lose track of reality.
It obtrudes into poetry, where the word
encounters the unembellished, obstinate world.
A Venn diagram where nothing overlaps
but touches, barely, like a kiss in billiards.

61

To make the bestseller lists, you have to
imagine your readers accurately and cater
to them. Or you can, if you can afford to,
dream up a better audience, educated,
sophisticated enough to appreciate
wit.... In short, your kind of people. (They may
exist in small numbers: the rare birds
ornithologists get up at dawn to glimpse.)

You'll never hear from them, though. Fan mail
is beneath them and anyway requires effort.
They are nonetheless to be admired
and as close as you are likely ever to come
to *simpatico* enthusiasts you deserve.
Meanwhile, sponge off your parents. Then marry money.

62

The words we say aloud indicate this
or that thing, serving us as servants
can and do. But there are words we cannot
say that have a power beyond our control.
For them we use a code: the "N" word
or the "F bomb." Sometimes acronyms
can cover them and yet convey their meanings,
obscene, profane, or insulting. They retain

the ancient nimbus many of their brothers
once possessed. Poets, at least the good ones,
try to restore to them the strength they've lost,
constructing a matrix of meter and maybe rhyme.
What their speakers risk is banishment
or stoning by the outraged, righteous mobs.

63

"*Autem, enim, igitur, demum, verum,*
quoque, also vocatives stand postpositive."
An utterly useless mnemonic! How often these days
do I find myself composing Latin prose?
Still, with it I do find myself.
A mental knickknack, it reassures me,
reminding me who I am. Frost used to say
he liked nightshirts because he could knock his knees

together and know that he was there (absurd
but also true). It's stored away in my mind
along with the Latin jingle: they affirm,
whenever I am in doubt, my identity.
Their uselessness (like that of poetry)
makes them heirlooms I cannot pass on.

64

A worn washer will do it: the water keeps going
but in slo-mo, so you have to wait
for each drop to form at the end of the spigot
and grow slowly, but holding on until
its weight is too much for the surface tension
to bear, and then the drop surrenders and falls.
So it is with an idea in the brain,
born through some imperfection and slowly growing.

To civilians—people, I mean, who are not writers—
it happens but they do not respond, would not
know how, and are not intrigued or challenged.
We have to turn away from these promptings, deny
them and ourselves, and feel their weight grow
until they can no longer hang on and they drop.

65

Antidepressants work well enough to get
a patient to feel better, more energetic,
and hoist again the burdens of life—the risk
being that with his vitality restored
he may remember the plan he'd made to escape
from his predicament, face up to the grim
truth he had discovered in his despair,
and cure himself by committing suicide.

The pills revive his pride, his self-respect:
no longer will he endure a torment he never
deserved. He will correct the world's injustice,
reassert himself, rebel, and kill
his persistent demon, however great the cost,
even if he is the one he condemns to death.

66

If a word were nothing more than its definition,
it wouldn't exist. It isn't its synonyms either,
but the letters, themselves, that hold the charm and the magic.
The Latin prayers and the Hebrew hide their meanings,
which are not anyway important. Understanding
is not the only or even the best approach.
Scholars forget that God was talking to shepherds,
not smart but wise and willing to sit and listen

as they had learned to do tending their flocks
to the twitter of birds, the barking of dogs, the screech
of owls in the night, or sudden silences
that demand more attention with their portents,
warnings that have no need of definitions.
The eloquence of our learned tongues is dumb.

67

Self-confidence is difficult to maintain,
especially for writers, who need to produce
a steady flow of venom—hatred, disdain,
and contempt for the stupidity, not only
of editors but of everyone, *tout le monde,*
we encounter on the streets, in elevators,
in buses, check-out lines in supermarkets,
the culture of the country, the country, itself.

Doubt (as any sane person would do)
even for a moment, and the arrogance
it takes to be a writer cracks a little.
In time—after the first assault, and there will be
more—the fissures deepen and ramify,
increasing the risk you run of total ruin.

68

Dada-ist merchandising? Certainly that,
but the pet rocks spoke to us somehow:
they were for conversation and never talked back.
(To reply is neutral, but talking back is hostile,
which is another example of how hard
English is for foreigners to learn.)
The rocks never made errors in grammar
or diction and never imposed with stupid opinions.

They never took any vows of silence. Rather,
it was their nature, as were modesty, reverence,
and tranquil acceptance. How did they achieve that?
They could not explain themselves but offered
their examples for us to emulate.
The fad is over: still they persevere.

69

Ask Galileo how much the church knows,
and he'll try not to laugh: the earth moves!
It's difficult to take their disapproval
of suicide more seriously than the threat
of hell (which would be worrisome if it existed).
The people who run bury patches dislike
notorious criminals, whose graves attract
crowds—as suicides' do not anymore.

The earth moved again when the Enlightenment
became the new religion and self-slaughter,
another martyrdom. Go out at night
and dig in the earth beneath crossroads to find
the dishonored bones of those who deserved better
(but disrespect was what they knew and expected).

70

New World monkeys with prehensile tails
can grab with them and hang high in the air.
Cows cannot do this, unless of course they are jumping
over the moon—as they may do in the daytime
when no one notices. This is not only not
writing but antiwriting, freed from the rules
of Wittgenstein's *Tractatus* that teaches us
how the world is everything that is the case.

Or that is *in* the case? Or the trunk or the hatbox?
What's necessary is in the *nécessaire*.
This is where thinking gets you—up in the air,
swinging from branches of imaginary
trees, which are almost everywhere, deep
in the rainforest, bedecked with many monkeys.

71

In book production, there was a time when changes
became expensive. You had in your hand page proof,
but would they have to reset a line or two?
A whole page? Pages? Your editor
sympathized, but bookkeepers mattered more
than books: you had to wait for a second edition,
if there ever was one. Could you believe Lazarus's
story but with Jesus doing it twice?

With print-on-demand, there are now no first
editions and books don't go out of print
but revert to ideas of themselves like unborn souls
the best of whom, some people believe, refuse
to descend from heaven to plunge into the shimmer
of time and the flux of the world of material being.

72

Pound said, "Pull down thy vanity!" Nobody
asks what's with the "thy?" An affectation?
A donning of some nondenominational
clergyperson's robes? It resonates
as if he is preaching in some vaulted chamber.
It's a sermon, then, inveighing against pride—
if you can get that far. "Pull down thy pants"
pops up in my mind, a demonstration

that I have not altogether given way
to vaingloriousness. It has already been—
just as I have been, myself—pulled down.
All I have left in which to take pride now
is a hard-earned humility. A joke?
Yes, but not that simply. Nothing is simple.

73

Take a few steps back to change your perspective
and all your private discontents diminish,
or at least appear to. Welcome your worries' larger
implications—not merely psychological,
but environmental, also, and historic.
Look at what we have done to tundras, jungles,
the oceans' depths, even the air. . . . Our lives
are wrong, as some of us have begun to notice.

What can be done? Our leaders make it worse
day by day and hour by ruinous hour.
But suicide is trivial. Better try
to imagine what hermits think about—the end
of the species and new life forms, better adapted,
that do less harm perhaps. Or perhaps not.

74

Mass murders, plane crashes, pandemics:
we never say out loud what we are thinking,
wicked but also true—that this has not broken
the record, as without malice, we had hoped.
We have survived, and mankind will recover
its numbers. Our destiny is deferred.
We were ready, and are, but we must wait.
Still, our mourning customs are changing

from grief to relief and even approval. The dead
are no more lost than the rest of us will be
with our history of making intelligent mischief.
The earth may begin again, with walking fish,
snakes with legs and such transitional creatures,
not that we'll know or care one way or another.

75

Where was I? Where am I now? The poem
instructs me to ask such questions, even though answers
are of no interest to anyone, even myself.
Languages die. Dalmatian, I think, with only
half a dozen speakers years ago,
and all of them dead now. Did they quarrel
and no longer talk to one another? The last
dreamt in Dalmatian, perhaps. Did firehouse dogs

learn to sit, stay, and fetch in a language
no humans knew anymore? Border
Collies obey hand signals but not Dalmatians.
In their brains, those mysterious phonemes remained
from shepherds they never knew in quaint costumes
we can imagine—and who would dare correct us?

76

Back to square one, which is not the same
as one squared, even though the result
appears so. There are elegant shortcuts
numbers can offer to those who are alert:
4% of 75 equals
75% of 4, easier
to compute (3). No mathematician, I
observe the dance of these agile, abstract

figures that leaves me blinking, a child again.
Innocence, which I sometimes think I remember,
can be almost as good as understanding
with its sneaky corollary, pride,
as if I knew much more. Limitation
can be an invitation. Or wisdom itself.

77

Only if I wasn't thinking about it
or seemed not to be thinking about it and crept
up behind it to grab it quickly could I
find a poem. They are elusive prey.
Now that I don't think about them at all
(or less than I used to) they creep up on me,
so that I am obliged to shoo them away
like pests, except that I have become the pest.

It isn't a trick. The poems are sly and know
whether one's lack of interest is real or feigned—
not that there is anything wrong with feigning,
which is an art also and takes talent,
but a different talent, difficult to learn—
even the rudiments—as I have discovered.

78

Does no one else in the hen coop notice
that our numbers diminish every day? The rooster's
crow is a dirge or, more likely, a warning
for us all to flee at once, flee for our lives.
But put a box next to the chicken wire
and not one in a thousand years will think
to jump up on the box and then over
and out. And if that's the case, we deserve to be killed

and even spatchcocked, which is Tudor-brutal
(but some elaborate recipes demand it).
Self-loathing is elementary, easy.
We graduate, some of us anyway, to a higher,
truer truth, having learned to despise
our entire species. And life itself.

79

If this were real, I should be looking it over
to see what I'd said and where it might be trending.
Long enough now to be a book—but what
does it mean (did I mean)? I'm proud to say
nothing whatever. Think of the frog's leg
electric stimulation can make twitch
even though the frog itself is dead
and no more will a-wooing go. Just so,

these are twitches, and I pronounced myself
dead some time ago. That this can happen
is curious and perhaps sad. (Disgusting?)
But it doesn't mean much except to the student
at the lab bench who keeps the charges going,
fascinated and probably also cruel.

80

The hand that is no longer there is clenched
tight or so the nerves report. (They know
no better.) Pain medication works sometimes,
and mirrors in which the eye contends with the part
that's missing. Never mind neurology,
this is a nice epistemological problem
philosophers love to play with among themselves.
The mirror therapy over time can help,

but in the glass I can no longer see
the look—even a faded one—of a poet.
It's only a sad old man with phantom pain
for which there is no relief. The writing hand
is too well trained to let go of the phantom
pen it clutches, taking silent dictation.

81

Neither great nor terrible, Somerset Maugham
was workmanlike, which is exactly on point.
A villa on Cap Ferrat and a study to die for.
His desk in front of a window with the blue
expanse of the Mediterranean before him
was an attractive idea, but Willie discovered
that there was nothing new to say to the sea
at which he kept staring. He rearranged

the room so that he faced a blank wall
and could ignore the seascape now behind him.
The view for any writer turns out to be
interior and portable. And cheap.
But cynics can be beguiled: a panorama
degenerates to a banal idea.

82

Are you still reading? Why would anyone do that?
Obsessive compulsive behavior, so that you feel
wicked if you leave a book unfinished?
Has your education taught you nothing at all?
Don't let me keep you. If you abandon me now,
I'll feel no loss. A figment disappearing
can be read as a sign of returning health. *Gezundheit!*
I do not recall signing any consent form

and assert (again?) my right to refuse treatment
and even to discharge myself, AMA.
They note this in my chart, not for my sake
but to protect themselves against lawyers
(the patient's or his heirs') eager to make—
excuse the phrase—a killing from the death.

83

Consent was not, as we once supposed, the end
but only the start of the game we used to win
regularly. But then the losses—at first
humiliating. (You learn humility's lessons.)
Eventually, you stop, but still the process
repeats itself each time you unscrew the cap
of the fountain pen. You're going to bed again
in the hope of a pleasure you know risks chagrin.

Will sentences come, or phrases? Single words?
Or after the little while politeness requires
will you replace the cap and walk away,
admitting once more that you've been a fool
to test yourself this way? Or shall we call it
more bluntly an old persistent habit?

84

We are taught to be wary of disinformation.
The truth cannot be blemished by our doubts.
It's the other way around with our pleasant fancies
not only dead but mourned. Who doesn't regret
the disengagement of storks from delivery rooms?
Are young children harmed in any way
by this fairy tale? Would they be better off
with illustrations in gynecology textbooks,

vivid as they are, candid and shameless?
What difference is there between polite white lies
and perjury? The motive is the same
—to improve upon the unsatisfactory facts
too difficult to bear. Or say, rather,
to imagine what would fix the broken world.

85

Just to be cautious, to rule out this or that,
and nothing to worry about . . . That's what the doctors
say, but the test is important enough to take.
The odds may be in my favor, but gamblers know
that even the most impressive run of luck
comes to an end. I will walk, sooner or later,
into the building but not out. Worry?
My prefrontal lobe works: of course I worry.

But all this brooding about suicide,
does it make sense? Is it mere flapdoodle?
Not necessarily. Ask me this afternoon
when I get back. I may have changed by then
and the answer also. Living is easy enough,
but thinking about it honestly can be hard.

86

Out in the super-boonies there must still be
diners with booths and round stools at the counter
where one can sit and watch the impromptu ballet
of the grill-man, cooking five orders at once,
omelettes, burgers, pancakes, fries, flipping,
while keeping track of the time for this food or that.
In their code, hardly in use anymore,
"86" let the servers know—

and nobody else—that they were out of something
(because it rhymes with "nix"?). The number has
a baleful resonance for those old enough
to have heard it called aloud. But what am I out of?
A great many things but, most important, time.
There is not much left. I am 86.

87

The bottle washes up on the sandy beach
of the castaway's island. Inside is a note
he extracts and opens to read. Nothing is there.
Were there words that faded? Can that happen?
Could it be a prankster, sending out
dozens of bottles with pieces of blank paper?
Or is there more to it? Does it demand
from each of us that he must write his own

message/confession/prayer? Is it a challenge
to improve upon the silence? Or accept
the one that will sooner or later certainly come?
Every morning, these questions pose themselves
so that I don't go down to the beach anymore.
But it follows me, and the sand is everywhere.

88

The conventional number of piano keys are music's
universe. (Who has ever composed
for the big Bösendorfers with ninety-seven?)
We may never touch those extra notes
but the strings down there below the usual bass
resonate to color all the others.
After the sustain, the sounds, dispersed,
die, but what we heard and felt in our bones

was different, whether we could tell or not.
Our tympani quivered, playing background music
to life that dwindles away to burnish the silence.
Without their hammers ever striking our nerves,
those curious supernumerary keys
change and perhaps improve the piano's timbre.

89

Surgery? Radiation? Nothing?
What are the odds? What I want is not
mere time but tolerable time,
and all they have is guesses and mumbo-jumbo
(Greek they have learned to use to intimidate
peasants not sufficiently impressed
by the endorectal coil). In frank English
my case is dire, my choices are all unattractive

and unimportant. What matters now are the smaller
decisions I have to make. Do I want to show
impatience anymore? Politeness is less
strenuous and often more effective.
It isn't me, but characteristics change,
or I can edit the fiction I have become.

90

In the social contract, there ain't no sanity clause,
and the puzzle to unlocke is how it applies
to those of us who are about to die,
the *morituri*, immune for a time to the harsh
penalties of the law. Why don't we use
this freedom to do some good in the world, kill
this villain or that? (Or the merely annoying
like those on the Mikado's little list.)

The answer is that we don't care anymore,
or not enough to bestir ourselves. Our ambits
shrink by the week. We no longer right wrongs,
or even write about them. Our thinking turns
objective and we live as objects do,
calm and indifferent to what no longer concerns us.

91

The Tavannes on my desk runs four minutes fast
in twenty-four hours, and I have to reset it
every morning: time stops and gives back
the few minutes so every day becomes
the end of a mini-daylight savings time,
and I can entertain the pleasant notion
that I may now live a few breaths longer.
But do these little gifts combine to give me

a few more sights and sounds for the black hole
to devour? Still, they will have existed
in an immutable time-past as particles
or waves do. Can we construct a belief
in anything more reliable and substantial?
There is nothing less, except nothing.

92

The news changes but the commercials don't,
the demographic being what it is—
old people, who have their aches and pains:
constipation, apnea, heartburn.
To them big pharma iterates its pitch
so often that we are bored more than afraid
(except that we're always afraid if we are conscious).
We check for symptoms, and sooner or later find

something to worry about. The diagnosis?
Uncertainty, and the treatment is watchful waiting—
that no one collects or marches for. We'll know
sooner or later if it's an illness or merely
the human condition on the world's ward. No flowers
or get-well cards, not yet. They will come later.

93

If the plans were more precise or if the stem cells
followed more closely the chromosomes'
instructions, would we be better off? Those minor
imperfections are where our identities lie,
ashamed, defiant... What's to be proud of?
What are vanity's grandiose claims about?
It takes a lifetime—often more—to face
modesty's imponderable question

that ripens slowly to reveal itself.
We are all slight seconds: how can we not
sympathize with one another, condole,
and study forbearance? The only prayer we need
to recite over and over apologizes
for what we are, have been, and have done.

94

A useful book of poetry? Indeed!
A textbook for creative writing classes
with the one essential lesson—in a word,
no. Don't even think about it. Suppose
colleges gave academic credits
for diseases: would you hurry to sign up?
(There is always a waiting list!) But look
at the adjunct lecturer, who publishes

to add to his or her CV and keep
the job that mostly involves the difference between
"to," "two," and "too." It's uncreative
writing, merely correcting grammar and spelling,
dull, but exactly what the students need
to carry out those jobs they will settle for.

95

Beating a dead hobbyhorse? Again?
What's the point? But what would be the point
in cutting it out or trying to improve it?
To make such repairs would be to betray
inadequacies, which are more truly mine
than any of the skills I've labored to learn.
The authentic me broods that the poet's trade
is irrational and ought to be avoided,

and the teacher's job is even worse, but you can't
let the students read your face to see
your disgust. If they did, they'd learn
nothing whatever—except that you are rude
and cruel. But so is the world they haven't chosen
but have to live in anyway. That's the point.

96

Dr. Johnson on Lord Lansdowne's poems:
"aspirations without ability."
Happens a lot, but to be remembered only
for one dismissive phrase? That's hard luck.
If naked aspiration is a joke
we all have the right to laugh at, still allow
in the poor baron's pretensions a sincere
regard for the art. He may have lacked talent

but he couldn't help not being any better.
Sometimes he may even have guessed and worried.
Honesty hurts without the help of the only
anodyne—stupidity, which I wish for.
Or wish I could wish for—except that this
formulation is not quite stupid enough.

97

Phishing, scams, identity thefts, and the passwords
designed to protect us (that don't work very well)
make sitting down at the desk a risky business,
although I wonder who would want to be me.
Not rich enough to be worth stealing from,
I'm old enough to be an unsuspicious
and therefore gullible mark, easy pickings.
And they, meanwhile, turn out to be colleagues,

inventing fictions designed for me to believe
and to get me to send Postal Money Orders
or Western Union's—art in its meanest genre.
It does take talent: they have to devise a tale
both plausible and sad enough to persuade me
for a few minutes. But I won't send them money.

98

Nothing this morning, which is a good sign:
I may be released from bondage or the ropes
have slackened a little. This is how normal people
are able to pass their days, facing banal,
uninteresting difficulties to which
there is no need to add. I am not
free, not yet, but there can be days when the burden
is less oppressive. What wouldn't Sisyphus give

for a day off to rest and glare up
at that cursèd hill? Or more modestly think
how they keep track at AA of the days—
some easier, some harder—they've managed
as they share with each other coffee, donuts,
and their pathetic stories, their epic pains.

99

The patient is feeling better, but the shrink
is not convinced. Spurious improvements
are common enough so there is a technical term
describing these poor souls as "fleeing to health."
Does it make a difference what the psychiatrist thinks?
Or is it just his guess, no better than yours?
His "door is always open." The pills work well.
If it isn't a cure, it's at least a remission,

but that does almost as well—not forever
but for much of the time that remains before you.
A flight into health is also away from madness,
depression, and a painful vision that may
or may not be true. But truth, health, and life
are abstract notions, not worth bothering with.

100

In the end, it is about the ends, not this one
or that, but all of them, the tyranny
of finitude against which we all rebel.
That's the appeal of suicide—we assert
for ourselves the right to determine when and how.
There can be odd moments of transcendence,
or at least denial, but if God is gone,
poetry, music, and even sometimes, paintings

afford us glimpses of something other and maybe
better. Without such brief encounters, life
would be—and indeed is—too much to bear.
Ideas are not enough; you need the words
to chew on (and numb you) so you can believe,
and, however baselessly, keep going.

INDEX

A manuscript remains passive until, 58
A paragraph signals a pause; a more emphatic, 1
A skein is a sixth of a hank, but that is not, 24
A useful book of poetry? Indeed!, 94
A worn washer will do it: the water keeps going, 64
A writer's silence is different from anyone else's., 32
After I've peed in the morning, I have to decide, 25
Ah, Percy, Percy, how do you feel, 54
Among the many reasons not to write, 56
An assertive dropped initial raises its voice, 2
An audience—an interview with a pope, 36
Anna, Dostoevsky's second wife, 52
Antidepressants work well enough to get, 65
Are rats ever wrong, abandoning sound, 26
Are you still reading? Why would anyone do that?, 82
As writing seems less attractive, one turns, 8
Ask Galileo how much the church knows, 69
"*Autem, enim, igitur, demum, verum*, 63

Back to square one, which is not the same, 76
Bad habits are hard enough to break, 35
Beating a dead hobbyhorse? Again?, 95
"Better coffee a Rockefeller's money can't buy," 55

Circular staircases and chandeliers, 7
Concentrate on your breathing. After a time, 23
Consent was not, as we once supposed, the end, 83

Dada-ist merchandising? Certainly that, 68
Does no one else in the hen coop notice, 78
Doubt is not your enemy: learn to embrace it, 27
Dr. Johnson on Lord Lansdowne's poems:, 96

Even if it makes no sense, one must, 4

German was Paul Celan's *Muttersprache*, 33
Graffiti artists, unlikely theoreticians, 18

How can I trust my friends' approval? What else, 28
How do those dragons guarding their treasure know, 37

I am pretending to write, or do I pretend, 45
I can remember how the growing pile, 41
I had given her up, but she persists—, 50
If a word were nothing more than its definition, 66
If all magicians are fakes, the best of them, 17
If the plans were more precise or if the stem cells, 93
If this were real, I should be looking it over, 79
In book production, there was a time when changes, 71
In the end, it is about the ends, not this one, 100
In the social contract, there ain't no sanity clause, 90
Is there any difference between writing, 51

Just to be cautious, to rule out this or that, 85

Kleist had been thinking about killing himself, 57

Mass murders, plane crashes, pandemics:, 74

Neither great nor terrible, Somerset Maugham, 81
New World monkeys with prehensile tails, 70
Not noble. Just an attempt to escape, 39
Nothing this morning, which is a good sign:, 98

On the one hand, the executives running Ford, 49
Only if I wasn't thinking about it, 77
Out in the super-boonies there must still be, 86

Painting = paint, canvas, and brushes, 21
Phishing, scams, identity thefts, and the passwords, 97
Pistols make noise . . . But would I hear it?, 5
Pockets: no longer having to carry things, 11
Pound said, "Pull down thy vanity!" Nobody, 72

Refinement? Sensitivity? In a pig's, 43
"*Risus sardonicus*" refers to the facial convulsions, 31

Self-confidence is difficult to maintain, 67
Shrouds are good manners, for none of the ghosts, 16
Socrates taught us all how little we know, 3
Some books pretend, or we pretend, 10
Spoiler alerts warn off the wrong readers, 12
Stage fright poses impertinent, pertinent questions, 19
Surgery? Radiation? Nothing?, 89

Take a few steps back to change your perspective, 73
Texts only seem to refer to something, 47
The bottle washes up on the sandy beach, 87
The conventional number of piano keys are music's, 88
The day always began with yesterday's work, 40
The Four Seasons in Philadelphia looks, 15
The Grand Guignol in Paris closed its doors, 20
The hand that is no longer there is clenched, 80
The news changes but the commercials don't, 92
The patient is feeling better, but the shrink, 99
The Tavannes on my desk runs four minutes fast, 91
The words we say aloud indicate this, 62
Thousands, tens of thousands have given up, 29
To be a writer! I used to think that made me, 42
To make the bestseller lists, you have to, 61
To stop writing is perilous. Late mornings, 9
Trollope's greatest fiction was the one, 46
"Truth to tell" is awkward, as it should be, 44

Was it Jeremy Bentham or John Stuart Mill, 48
We are taught to be wary of disinformation., 84
We can endure most disappointments, losses, 59
We learn words first and then the grammar, 30
We used to read to learn what the world is like, 13
Weightlessness is a diminution of being., 53
What do you do with a royalty check for ZERO, 60
Where should a novel stop? How and when?, 34
Where was I? Where am I now? The poem, 75
While Friedrich Rüchert, the eminent scholar, was working, 14
Writers invent things. It's part of the job., 38
Writers kill themselves, not all but enough:, 6

You're reading along and you come across a word, 22

Milton Keynes UK
Ingram Content Group UK Ltd.
UKHW031306041024
2011UKWH00041B/183